A Call From Me, To Me

Manisha Mahajan

First published in India in 2016 by Invincible Publishers

ISBN: 978-93-86148-01-8

Invincible Publishers

F-55, Sushant Lok II, Hong Kong Bazar Lane Sector 57,
Gurgaon-122003

Opposite Kasturba Ashram, Radaur Distt Yamuna Nagar,
Haryana- 135133

Acknowledgement

I have been a seeker in my present life and have strived to find a Living Master, who would guide me through. My wish was fulfilled last year, when I came in touch with Master Raj and the Breathwave Foundation.

This journey has been an eye opener of sorts. It has opened up new vistas about my own self, many of which I did not know existed in me. Being on this path, I constantly strive to better myself every moment.

I am deeply indebted for the blessings, teachings and the constant presence, on each step of the way. Thank you Master, Latha teacher and all the soulmates of my Breathwave family.

This mortal journey is filled with experiences both good and bad, but I believe our perspective on life labels them. Every soul who has walked footsteps with me on this journey has held value for me. Knowingly or unknowingly, they have paved the way to make me the person I am today, as also helped me understand the purpose of my life.

I would like to thank each one of them, for teaching me, in ways, which they thought was appropriate for me, at any given point of time.

I humbly bow to what my parents, Late Dr. M.L. Goyal and Dr. (Mrs.) Santosh Goyal, did for me in their lifetimes and beyond.

My two lifelines: my daughters, Kriti and Navi, without whom life would lose meaning. I cannot thank them enough for always being there. My very best of friends, my guides and my best critiques.

A very special thanks to Mohit, from whom I have learnt to see life in a different perspective and view my life changing decisions in a new light.

A special thank you to my brother, Mayank and sister-in-law, Supriya for being there at each step.

Deeply indebted to Raju and Chumani, without whose love and care, I would never have been able to pursue my passion.

And, of course, to my four legged babies, Scruffy, Chester, Chotu and Snoopy, who taught me how to love unconditionally.

Preface

How does one write or paint or dance or compose music? Is it just a means to unleash our creativity or does it have a deeper meaning to it? Does it make us connect to who we are, at the very source?

We are travellers here and we seek to fulfill ourselves by doing what we are best at. This pursuit of finding what we do best leads to the inception of any piece of art. For some, it may be a beautiful dish, for others' a new car design or an ikebana ensemble.

The verses in this book have found inspiration from such people, in all walks of life. People who are struggling to find their identity, people who have been lucky to find it but are unable to express it and lastly people who have the will to struggle anymore. We all have latent qualities and through this book, I would urge each one of you to look for the lotus within. Dive in deeply, through the muck, the layers and find what you truly are. For, each one of us has very few moments in every existence as a human.

Gratitude

Who am I, if not but a speck in your divine presence
A bud, waiting to bloom
A life, waiting to sprout

From where I look,
You are found everywhere
In the elements which form
This very existence
From where I look,
Your luminosity is shining
And, my eyes cannot contain
From where I look,
Your presence is felt
In every pore
From where I look,
You are the very existence
From where I look,
You are within me
Engraved on my being.

From where I look
Master, you, I see
Only you,
With my closed eyes
In wonderment
A mortal,
In your immortal presence.

Seasons

As the winter sun warmed up my painful fingers,
I felt comfortable in sitting here
Slowly, the blood started flowing in my veins.
I could feel the gushing,
As I tried to balance my emotions,
With the speed of the blood.

Here I was silently gazing atthe not so green lawns,
The few people sitting and chatting,
With not a care in the world.
Or maybe,
This was the human way of tackling with the mundane stuff
Looking for ways to caress one's soul
Letting go sometimes to the surroundings
Looking for ways and means, to bring ourselves out of our own reality
Life itself shows us a plethora of colors,
Which we are supposed to define many a time,
Failing mostly and succeeding sometimes.
This game keeps on playing in each one of us.
We call this life. Yes we do.
But, coming back to the winter sun,
How everything in life is a paradox,
Relative to each other.
The summer sun is harsh or the winter sun warm.
A thought in our mind,
And, it is just that.

Relative to all, duality in all.
Where am I in this?
Do I exist in this duality?
Or do I go beyond the seasons,
The warm or cold does not play on me.
I am in balance with the world inside me.

The Coral Jasmine

For whom do I bloom?
Only at night
My life melts away, in a moment
I fall from my abode, in sorrow,
Of waiting for a loved one,
To look into my soul,
My beauty unparalleled
I regale in my fragrance,
Which is like the deer
Who carries the musk
Far and wide
Look not for me on the branches,
For I am found only in the mud below,
That is where I am,
Before I pass on into oblivion
My birth is in quick succession of my death,
And my death makes me born again
At the same place,
At the end of the night,
When you see the horizon,
You will feel my fragrance,
In the whiff of the air which reaches you.
In your waking,
Will be my death
In your sleep,
My birth
For that is our destiny,
And, beyond this circle of life and death,

We will be only one
We always were
Sacred in our beauty,
Rare in our fragrance
Like the musk deer.

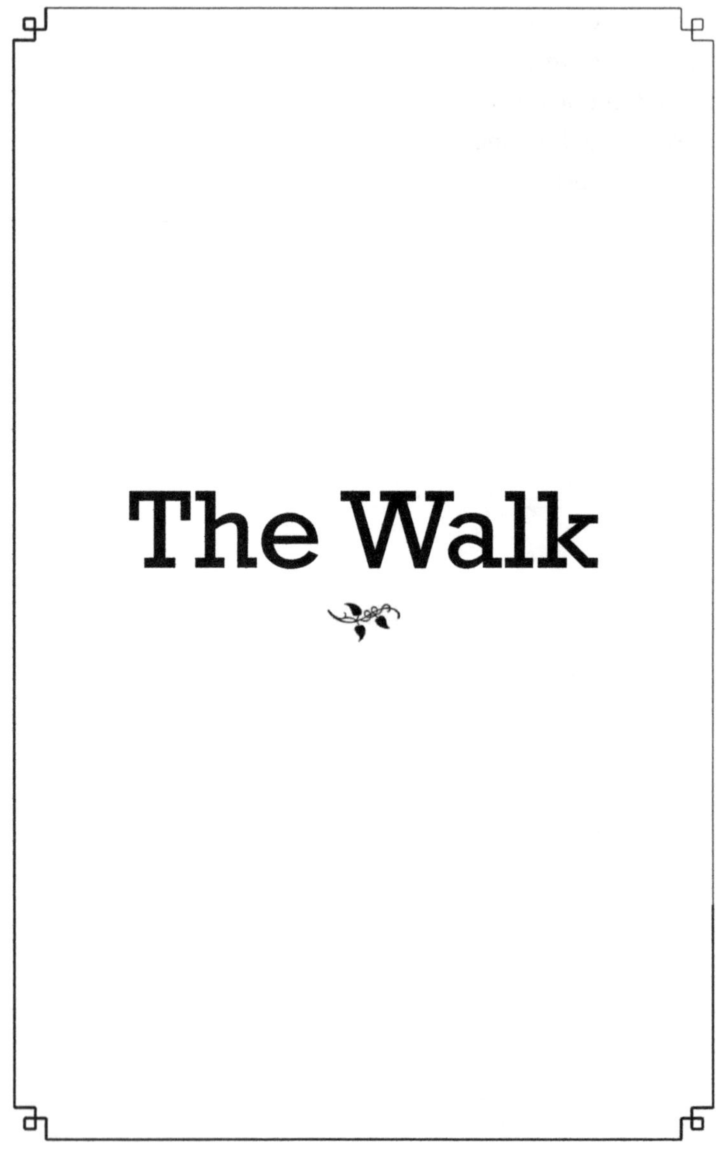

The Walk

I travel along the cobbled path,
With the quaint little houses
All with the painted red roofs,
In the little winding lanes
Where history speaks in many words,
In silence...
The walls have their own story to tell
The flowers lined up on the window sills
Bloom merrily in the fresh autumn air
I travel along,
As many have travelled along this pathway
Of yearning, of learning
Of hope, of desire
Of love, of helplessness
Of lost worlds, of unknown lives
I travel along,
No destination in mind
None there anyways
I travel along,
In the present
As history passes me by
As a spectator
As a watcher
Many journeys taken
Many journeys left
I travel along,
In the hope to find the treasure

For which I had left home
I travel
To find
What I had left at home.

Thoughts

Sitting in the morning sun,
In the midst of the pines and the oaks,
I reflect back, on the years gone by
People say that, they have had carefree childhoods,
Or happy marriages or good lives
What I find is, how foolishly we try to fit ourselves
Into the others definition of thought and perception
We have only ours to see
And, as I reflect back today,
I realize, that my journey was always about me
There never was another,
There never will be.
And, I also realize,
The meaning of relationship is singular
We only make it plural.

Nature

The skies were overcast
Casting a dull hue on the trees,
The birds were chirping furiously,
Giving their loved ones a warning
Rain, anytime
Looking afar, into the trees
I seemed to blend,
As the green enveloped me,
Hugging me tightly,
Telling me I am here now.
With you.
The drizzle on the soil
The wetness of the earth
The branches bowing down
As if praying, in gratitude,
Surrendering to the universe
To the existence.
Stillness.
How strange, that the overcast skies
Have always been likened
To a depressive state
That is who we are
A different view, a different lifetime
Relative.
Dual.

Ownership

You think you own the earth,
On which you build your abodes,
Your castles, your domes?
You think you own that part of the land where you reside,
For which you pay millions?
Do you own that money, made of paper?
Is not the paper made from the wood,
Which comes from the trees?
Do you own the trees as well?
What is really yours?
The forests, the soil, the air, the sea, the ocean
What do you really own?
And, you think you have achieved!
You have lost everything.
You have lost the very purpose of your existence
You have lost your own self in this self-created mirage
You have lost.
But, still you sleep on feather soft mattresses,
Dreaming of ways to amass more paper.
Dead you are, like the paper.
What you think you own,
Has been owned by millions,
And,
Will be owned by more
You are no one,
So live like no one.
For you are nothing.

In Silence

To sit in the sun, listening to the birds
Sweat slowly trickling down, following gravity
My fingers entwining a leaf, not realizing
The game of hide and seek being played by the squirrels,
searching for food.

The Crow croaking at each and every one
The sound of the school bus,
Honking away, lost in the animated chatter of children
The workers furiously peddling away,
To reach work on time
The dead leaves of the tree,
Trying to hang for dear life
The parched roofs of the buildings,
Standing tall in the heat
The passerby,
Taking timeout to drink water from the roadside stand
The shrill bell of the vegetable vendor,
Spreading hurriedness in the house
The cacophony and the smells,
Emanating from the kitchen,
Furiously churning up the day's meals
The petals of the flower,
Stretching out to bloom
The ash lying,
After the heat burned down the hut
The co-existence,
With matter

I, a part of this existence,
Merge with the surroundings
I, cease to be,
I
For, nature is me, and I am her
We have both a parasitic and a symbiotic relationship.

The Tree

The tree looked away, beaten and dejected,
Cold, as the winter breeze blew,
Hurting it to the core,
As the blanket of leaves had long shed away.

How was the tree to understand this change of season?
But, the moon looked on,
As if trying to warm the bare limbs,
A love with no words,
Not seen in us mortals,
Who die in the process of love, yet,
Fail to learn the art
The art of no conditions,
Of being there
Just being there
But, then, the moon is no mortal like us.

The Pathway

The pebbles on the path,
Gave me a sense of direction
Asymmetrical,
Yet in symmetry
Making a tapestry
Meandering along the banks
With the curvature of the river
The river flows,
A destination unknown.
Taking the help of the little stones,
Though insignificant
Yet there, visible.
The focus lies on the flow,
Not on the little flags,
Deciding its course.
The pebbles in their stillness are mute, unhurried, just there
Aiding in their own way,
As if willing, prodding, egging to go on…
Wish I was like the pebble
Letting the river be on its way
Aiding, yet unaided.

The King

The sun played hide and seek,
Through the thick vines
It was nature's abode
Everything was in harmony,
The circle of life complete
I waited, in the nook of a tree,
In all preparedness
To pounce
For I had not eaten in a week
Suddenly the silence shattered
A gun shot.
Not natural at all
In a distance, I saw
A goat running for dear life
I, the king of the jungle, was dumb
I took flight to catch
Little did I know
That this was to be
A daily practice
So that the exclamations could come out of the tiny mouth
Which was well fed.
And, I would be made in to a documentary.

I See

I see...
I see you in the sequined frock,
With the little smocking done at the yolk,
The many frills cascading from your slender waist,
Your hair in an unkempt mess,
The pink of the frock matching the glow on your cheeks.

I see you in the pristine white school dress,
Waiting in anticipation for the school bus,
Waving goodbye,
Getting on to the next step.

I see you, graduating,
In the black overalls, embarking on a new platform,
With matching earrings,
The kaleidoscope of colors around you.

I see you as a resplendent bride,
In all the finery, with stars in your eyes,
Conquering new horizons.

I see you, as a mother,
A little one in your arms,
Fulfilled, complete.

I see you, turn into a woman,
A woman full of love, a woman of strength,
A woman of substance
I see you, turn into me, partly.

I see you..
I think I know you,
Inside you

But, do I really see you.

You have metamorphosed into a star in the horizon.
And, I am standing at the same place,
With the pink frock,
Sequined, embedded in my heart.

Unborn

Why was I born,
If not to be
In control of the vultures around me
To be sniffed out at birth?
Or like a piece of meat,
Butchered?
Or in a harem,
At the beck and call of the self-proclaimed masters?
Or under a veil, unable to breathe ?
Or to be hit inside the closed doors,
Never letting out a cry?
Was this God's sense of humor?
Or is this man made?
Were not the seven vows,
About the rights and the duties,
When did the rules change?
I was made a prisoner,
With an invisible thread,
Which, I chose to be tied with
I guess.
Then,
That is why I was born
And, as always,
The fault is entirely mine.

My Daughter

My daughter wears short dresses,
But,
She got through the best business school
My daughter drinks,
But,
She is a Manager at twenty five,
In a blue chip company
My daughter smokes,
But,
She topped the university
My daughter knows how to cook,
But,
Chooses to rest when she is tired
My daughter believes in what she is,
And, I am proud of what she believes.
If you can walk beside her, good for you
For my daughter,
Will shine through,
With or without you.
For, I have not clipped her wings
And, believe you me,
Will not let anyone either.

Just Because

Just because,
I did not fill your coffers
Just because,
I did not behave the way you wanted
Just because,
I did not respect you enough as per your standard
Just because,
I did not fit into the mold you created for me
Just because,
I did not question you on your language
Just because,
I did not flinch when you hit me
Just because,
I did not show my tears when you dried me out
Just because,
I did not show my strength when you tried to
overpower me
Just because.
I let you be who you were..
I did not for once mean that,
You could turn me into you,
A self-eating monster
And, that is why,
I know the answer and you do not
That, I was full of love for you and for me
You were full of hate,
For you and for me.

The Black Sheep

You were dark and ugly,
You were stupid and slow
You were not up to the family standards,
You were told each day.

But, you were a child of God,
You felt beautiful inside.
You had wings and wanted to fly.
You took little steps
Trying to learn
Trying to fit in
But, slowly and steadily,
One by one,
Your wings were clipped.
Little did your innocent mind know,
That in the garb of your caretakers,
Live devils of their own making

You fought till you could
The onslaughts continued,
and, you thought, finally,
That, to fight more,
You had to become one of them,
Which you did.

It was a game of survival,
of the fittest,
You survived
By dying,
You won.

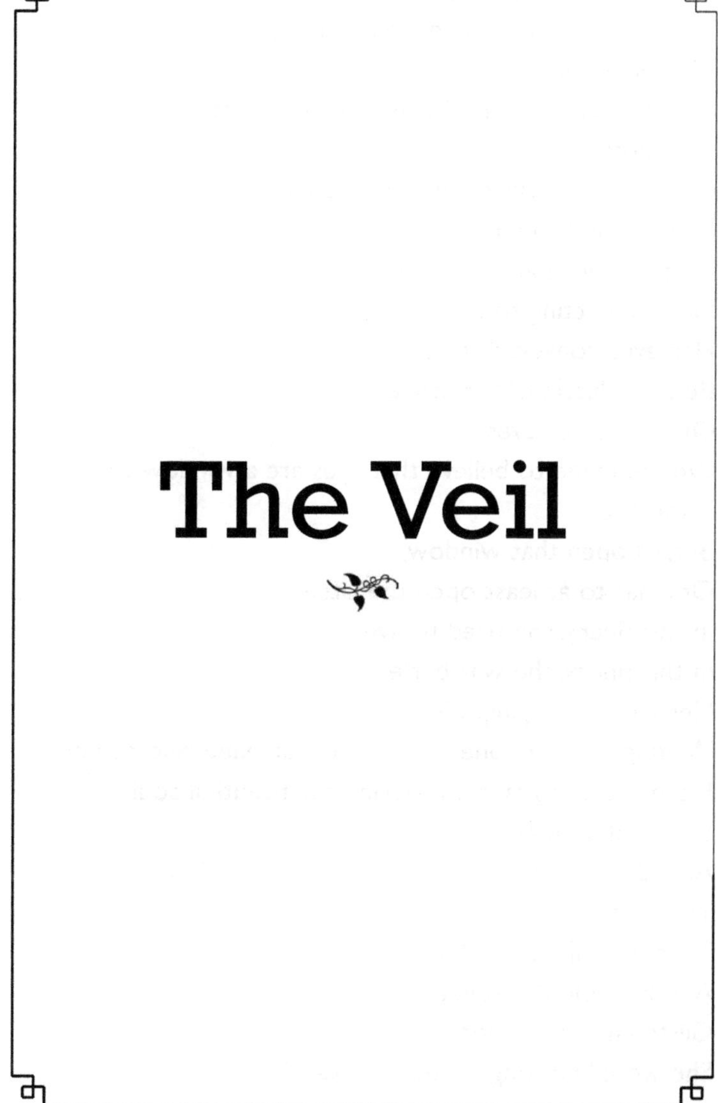

The Veil

Behind the veil of solitaires,
The Rolls-Royces', the private planes,
The jet set life,
Stood a person, scared and scarred for life
The target of all,
Garnering the envy and the jealousy,
From all and sundry
People looked at her varnishes,
Not connecting to her soul
Her eyes conveyed the pain,
But, the dazzle of the stones
Outshone her eyes
We are made to believe that eyes are a window to the soul
But, to open that window,
One has to at least open the latch
In this finery, she tried to live
In this finery, she was buried
Her eyes in longing, still
Waiting for someone to open the latchand release her,
From the many layers covering her beautiful soul
She lived in hope,
And, died in hope
To be born again,
Till her soul would shine,
And become the solitaire,
Glistening on its own
She would no longer need the varnish.

The Bride

In my bridal finery,
Resplendent as a bride,
I stood, happy, radiant.
With the layered walls of foundation,
My eyes blackened with kohl,
Waiting for the moment when
I would see the love of my life come past the veil,
And whisper the magic...
A word, a sentence, a meaning, a connotation
Which transports one into the land of bliss, in a millisecond.
But, what I saw from the corner of my eye
Was an apparition.
With blood shot eyes, reeking of liquor
With his set of fellow men, lewd and loud
I stood there, stupefied,
Glued to the landing.
Before,
I turned and walked down the steps
With my head held high,
The trail of the heavily embroidered lehenga,
Behind me.

Me

Closing my eyes I sat cross legged on the floor,
Trying hard to still my shaking body
The tears fell, like the
Rain Gods had opened up all their pent up emotions
And, it all came back
One by one, bit by bit
Me, an Olympic medal holder
Me, a topper
Me, a person of world fame
Me, successful,
Me, a guide for many
Me, a force to be reckoned with
Me, a person the world wanted to become
Yet, this me,
Could not win.
This me, failed.
This me, shed tears of helplessness today.
And this me,
Lost the battle within.
I failed me,
After winning over the world,
As I hung on the noose.

The Joker

I was always there, an extra.
Like the Joker in a pack of cards,
Always being fit in,
Here and there,
At the last moment,
A stop gap arrangement.
I was always there, a doormat,
No emotions of my own,
Nothing to feel, nothing to react to.
Trampled upon, laden with dirt.
I was always there, like the pawn,
On the chessboard,
One step forward, at the beck and call,
Of the kings and the queens
I was always there, the last one,
To be told to fit in, to adjust,
The stepney in the car
I was always there,
I was always there,
Till,
I could feel the warmth of the sun,
The fragrance of the rose,
The wetness of the rain,
Till, I became,
One with me,
The trump card,
Finally!

The Knowledge

Where you were coming from
I was aware, though not fully
Yes, you had a bad childhood
Yes, you were beaten and pulled
Yes, you were made the black sheep
Yes, you fell of the track
Yes, you had no friends
Yes, you were bullied
Yes, you were an overgrown child

But,
You were also intelligent
You were capable
You read
You wrote
You understood
You made it through
You became successful

So,
Who gave you the right
To live your bad childhood
All over again
Trying to fit your spouse into the
compartments of your challenges
Or your children into the picture frame of your lost
desires

As I said,
You were intelligent

Then, how did you not see
That to learn from your past
You need to embrace the present

But, I guess,
I was not fully aware
And still am not,
That, you were still that child,
In the body of a man
You could never grow up
And be a gentleman.

Am I You?

I started becoming like you
In the way you held your morning cup of tea,
The way you pressed the toothpaste to make it like an
ice-cream cone
The way you would get angry at the slightly burnt toast,
Or the elliptical roti
Or the less salt in the vegetable

I started becoming like you,
In ways that I could not fathom,
My expression, my behavior,
My response system,
My everything,
Became a mirror image of your way of functioning.
To the extent of the small line on the forehead,
When things did not go as per me.

I started becoming like you,
When and how I do not know?
But, when people started asking,
That are you siblings?
That is when,
Yes, that is when
I threw off the cloak,
Which had slowly turned me into you
For that was not who I was
I wanted to fly
And you wanted to be a bird,
Caged.

Love?

I thought it was love,
When I bared my soul to you

I thought it was love,
When I opened my scars

I thought it was love,
When I shared my dreams

I thought it was love,
When I showed my pain

I thought it was love.

But, for you, it was not love.
For you,
I was an object,
Of desire,
Of control,
Of slavery

Anything, but love.
You wanted to use me,
All of me
And then, throw me in the bin,
Like a use and throw piece
Or put me in the garbage sale,
As a seconds.
But, see the irony
I thought it was love,
Still,
When I let you
Use me.

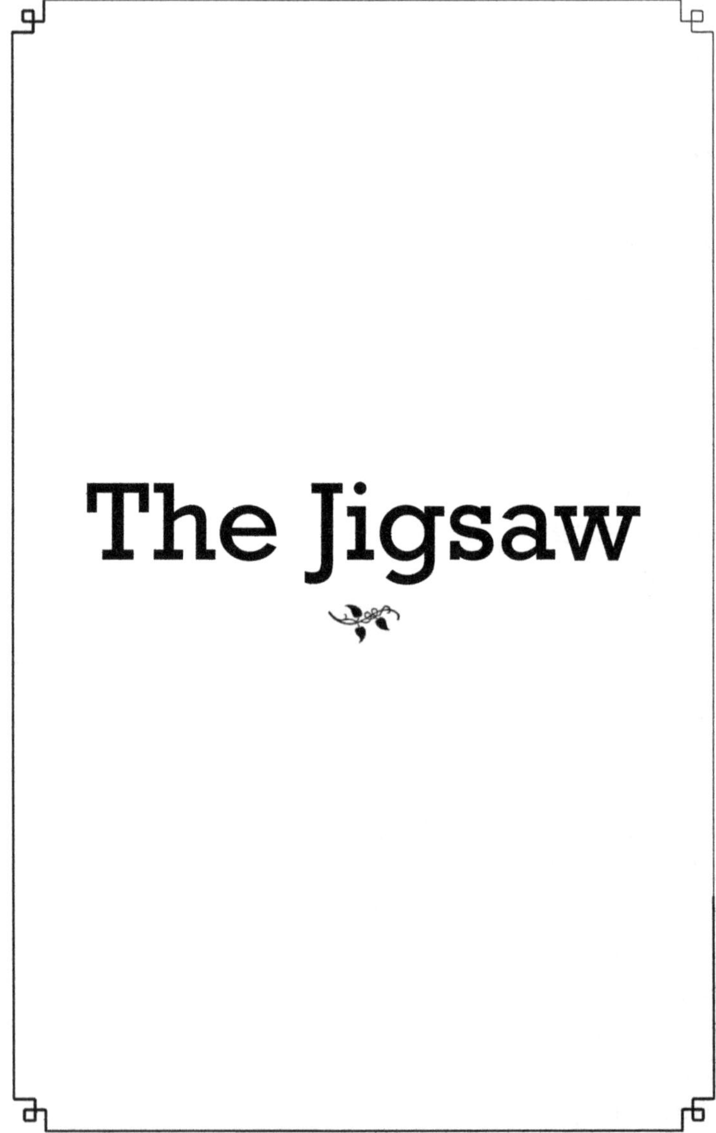

The Jigsaw

Your journey is yours to keep,
As is, your form, an extension.

How can I fit the pieces of this jigsaw of life?
Your domain remains yours,
As mine shuttles between yours and mine.
The need fulfills,
When the patterns in the kaleidoscope
Match the cracked bits in my domain.
Happiness comes in bits, as the pieces rearrange,
And I am left again, dejected
Trying to fit into a shoe that bites,
My need to be needed surfaces again,
And, sadly,
I, fall prey to it.

The Defective Piece

I was born with a manufacturing defect,
Or so, I came to know,
Neither did my family, nor my friends,
Were aware of this.
Suddenly, out of the blue,
This new designation was given to me,
Much like the coveted doctor, or her highness,
Poor me,
Yes, that was who I was,
So, in all my senses,
I accepted it.
And filled the crevices of my heart,
With the mundane and the sundry
I tried to mend and sew,
So that the defect could not be seen
To the outside world.
Without knowing what,
And where to mend and sew,
And lo and behold,
The gaps got filled, with gold;
Like they do in Japan,
When a pot gets broken, they fill it with gold,
The crack is visible, but, valuable,
For all to see.
Whatever impurities were there,
Got sifted away...
Thank you for calling me a defective piece
For, I was never one

But, in doing so,
You helped me repair my soul
So that, I could connect with myself,
And explore the real me.

No, I was never a defective piece
Nor did I have a manufacturing defect
You were impure
And, I,
Made myself pure, unwittingly,
Through you.
Thank you!!

Mother

However which way I choose to address you,
You always come to me with your heart wide open
Your heart is not filled with blood alone,
It is held together,
By the millions of hearts that you have stitched together,
Bit by bit,
And held steadfastly,
Over the generations
Your heart is an enigma,
To all and sundry
You think you live here in this mortal world,
But, you are made of the stars,
The universes and the galaxies,
And the many worlds there are,
For, you are someone,
Who even God bows down to,
For you are a Mother,
For you are the divine grace,
For which,
We mortals,
Look for everywhere,
Except in your heart.

In Harmony

As I walk along the pebble strewn path,
The sun plays along the crevices of the trees,
The water glistens,
Vying for my attention
Little birds come and sit on my shoulder,
As if questioning my presence
I hear the pitter patter of the squirrels,
Wanting a nut or two
The sky bows down to me,
With the clouds touching my feet
I am left, wondering,
That have I intruded into their world
Or have they completed mine.
I, an outsider,
In the flame filled forest,
With the snowcapped mountains,
With the shimmering gold beach,
Am I intruding?
Or do I really belong as one of them,
At peace, contained, inclusive
Yet exclusive, within.
For me to reach this understanding
Has taken lifetimes,
And, how many more
Have I travelled this path before?
Is this the past or the future?
Yet, I rejoice in the present
For nature itself, is God

Then, why wonder, that God is invisible.
I merge
With the divine
And become the grain of sand,
The cloud, the snow,
The squirrel, the ant
Complete, contained,
In harmony.

Bonding

Grant me the prerogative of bonding with you
How I bond with you is my choice.
For, my relationship with you exists in my head
You are not a party to this
I see you the way I want to see you
It does not matter to me,
Who you really are or how you see yourself.
How I see you, is the reality for me
I feed on that reality and build my armor on this base.
I treat you this way, because this is who you are,
For me.
Who you really are,
I don't know and I don't wish you knew either
You live with me, always
And cease to exist outside my world.
I define you my way,
You may define me your way
If we meet midway,
We are in love
If we do not,
We are in hate
But,
What if,
You are in love and I am in hate,
Or vice versa
How will we solve this equation?

The Fire

The fire died out
The smoldering pieces remained
With a little stick in my hand,
I prodded, breaking the symmetry.
Suddenly, some rekindled,
As if woken out of their reverie
The beautiful wood I had put,
Changed to coal, losing its identity
How simple, I thought.
And here I was,
Trying to pick up pieces,
Showing resistance in every thought, every moment
But the wood, changed to coal
About to disappear into the unknown,
Still rekindled, by a small push
Giving a spark of light, of life,
Fully, unquestioningly,
What a difference!
I am like the wood,
Or the coal
Or the flame
Or I am all of them.
I am or I am not.

The Treasured Wounds

What is it that you want to treasure?
If not the larvae infested wounds
Of yesteryears
And, let them become live with the current breeding
Some turning into pupas
Then, into the moths
No, and not butterflies
For butterflies, are a sign of beauty
And wounds, are a sign of grief
Of hurt, of dejection, of unfulfillment
Of lost hope
Yet, you want to keep them,
In the diamond crusted safe deposit boxes
With the velvet cushioned layers,
Satin glowing in between.

What is it you want to treasure?
Is it the treasure, the trapping?
Or is it the tar colored wound
Artificially dipped in the sandalwood?
Fragrant on the outside
And stinking on the inside
Bandaged,
With the frayed edges,
The yellow stains,
The dressed up wound,

Till when will you treasure?
Till it will have to be amputated

With a part of you
Till then?
Will you wait?
Till then?
Will you preserve your treasure?
And mummify it.
Because the air around will not turn it into a butterfly
Till you want it to,
Will you keep waiting?
For this metamorphosis?
The answer is in you.

The Travel

The journeys we have to partake,
Are always to be taken alone.
For, in birth or in death, it is our sole soul.
We may have fellow travellers along the way
Yet, we have to put out our own foot,
One after the other.
Unfailingly.
Though choices are there,
Yet, we are bound
In this trajectory of life,
To the unknown, to the lessor known, to the known,
We are mere dandelions, waiting to be flown,
By the next caress of the wind.
Yet, we must gather the strength, to put our next foot forward,
Our best foot forward.
In anticipation, that the next caress will take us closer to our destination.
Many miles to travel still,
Many miles to travel alone.
Undefeated, unfettered, unfazed,
Alone, yet, not lonely...
Anymore
Fulfilled, the cup overflows
Let the journeys keep happening
Let me go on,

No destinations, No stopovers,
No one else,
But, me.
With me.

Change

When we try and change our destiny,
We make a choice.
A choice towards the better.
To choose a lower suffering than a higher one
To tip the scales in our favour
To change the crests and the troughs
To reduce the depths and the heights
To gather our strength
To fight to live
A life, like a simple human being
Free,
And, not tied up, in the shackles of the so called relationships
Where one is treated like an animal
Where the fight is not to survive
But, to be subjugated
Till only the skeleton is left.
The only way to live is to be the strength itself
So that, the jackals of the mortal world, both outside and inside,
Can never strip you naked.
And bare you, of all your sensibilities
So, change
Change, being the only constant
Change and choose, the lesser of the suffering
And turn it on its head,
Don't choose happiness
Be it.

Judgment

Who are we to judge?
Life has its own plans
To put a newborn to sleep
Or to keep a decapitated person alive
To blow hot winds in already parched areas
To make it rain in severely flooded areas
Who are we to judge?
For life plans ahead of us
Not giving any intimation
Nor expecting us to retaliate
Who are we to judge?
For life is life.
It gives to take
It hits to shape
For life is life.
We still say, love the life you have
Instead, love the paradox of life
The duality which it projects
Who are we to judge?
For to love life, we have to love death
Who are we to judge?
Who are we?
Who?
Mere mortals, mere travellers
To end in a straight line after all
Existing in a limbo
Which we choose to call Time.

Pain, an emotion?

How many types of pain are there?
Is the pain by a pin prick, for measuring our blood sugar, the same when done by mistake?
Is the pain post-delivery the same as post-surgery?
Is the pain of losing a life the same as losing a limb?

How many levels of pain are there?
Is losing a child the greatest pain or losing a parent?
Or losing a spouse or failing a relationship,
Or failing yourself
How does one measure pain?
What is the threshold of pain?
Different for different people
What is pain, essentially?
If not, just a feeling,
An emotion,
Ingrained in us,
Like the many others,
On this shop floor?
It moves systematically, like a well-oiled machine
Like a supply chain
Sometimes,
It makes the system fail,
Sometimes,
It restructures the parts
Sometimes,
Rewiring is required
And,

Sometimes,
It changes the blueprint itself.
So, why blame the cancers and the others
When pain is the only one to blame.
Stop measuring pain.
Whether in the physical, the emotional, the mental or the spiritual
Stop defining pain.
Or,
It will keep on defining you
As it always has.
There really are no types of pain,
No levels and no measurements
Pain just is,
An integral part of our framework.
Our journey as a human,
Is to transcend the pain.

The Goal of Life

What is the goal, what is the destination?
Where to go, where to tread?
What to seek, what to learn?
There is infinity,
Both outside and inside
What does one want to achieve,
Or not to?
What is the trial or the tribulation?
Where are we going or coming from?
What do we know or not?
What or who are we?
A particle of dust, a pearl in the oyster,
A whiff of air, a drop of rain,
Invisible, yet there.
In inertia or in motion
Still or in stillness,
Existing now or forever?
Who?
What?
Where?
How?
Meaningless or meaningful.
We.
Just a juxtaposition,
Of words, of life, of existence.
Nowhere to go, nowhere to be.
But, here.
Now.

The Shiva Element

Who protects the little one?
The one who sleeps in a makeshift hammock?
Made out of a worn out cloth,
Near the mother, who toils at the construction site,
With big boulders on her head and dust all around
Yet the baby's smile is angelic.

Who protects the toddler?
Who sleeps under the highways?
With the daily grind of the tires,
And the maddening traffic,
Begging for his sanity.

Who protects the child, no more than ten?
Who rolls out cigarettes or incense sticks?
In the unlit factories,
Where breath is at a premium.

Who protects the young adult?
Who cycles early mornings to throw newspapers?
Or clean the cars, be it summer, rain or winter.

Who protects the adult?
Who works at the liquor stall or the makeshift eating joint?
Where guzzlers shout profanities every day.

Who protects the old man?
Who has been on the road,
Though, by now accustomed to this life,
But, is in denial and fails to accept.

Who is the protector and who is the giver?
Is everything destined, or our karma?

Who is the one on the street and who is the one, in the air conditioned house?
One who begs to live and one who lives with stardust
Are we essentially not made from the same five elements?

Who is his God and who is mine?
Am I not him and he, not me?
Who am I, if not born out of him, or he of me,
Are we not, but, peddlers on this earth,
Each selling our own wares,
To survive,
And, clueless about each other's journey.
The protector, the creator, the destroyer
All merge in me.
The Shiva element.

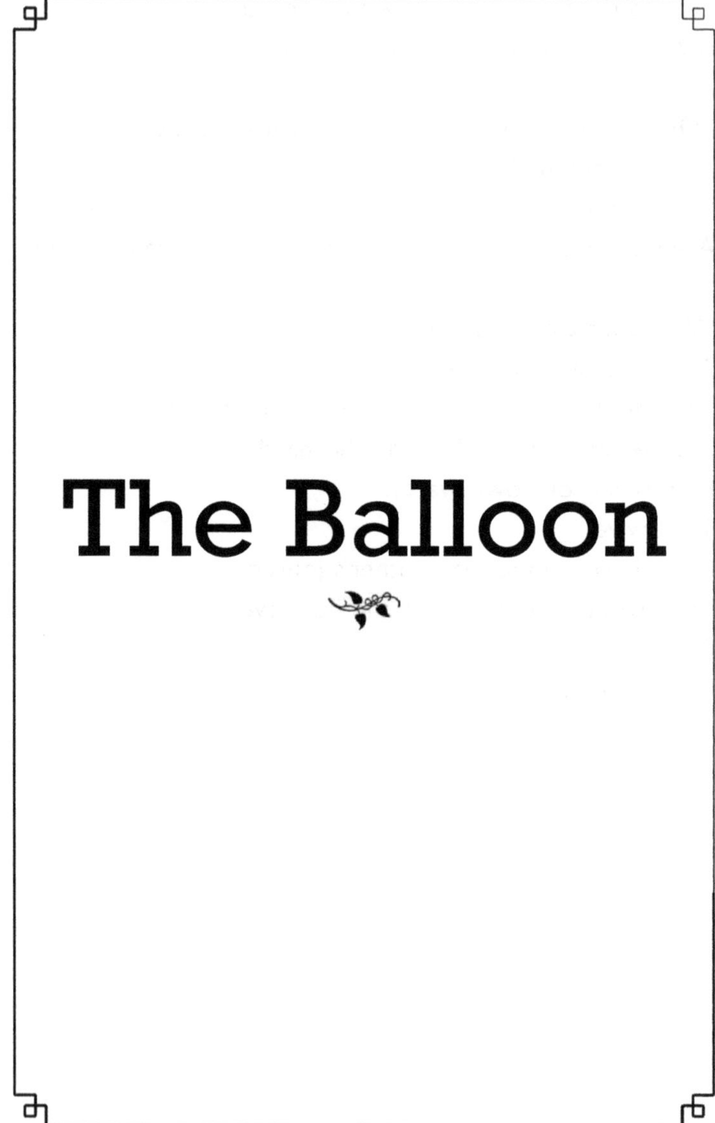

The Balloon

There he was,
The balloon seller,
With his colorful balloons,
Tied securely to his bicycle
In different shapes and sizes,
Filling dreams and wonderment in the little eyes,
With the helium.
I got the red horse,
The blue bird,
The yellow twirl.
Happy in my own world,
I pranced all the way home.
These were mine, my treasured possessions.
I ran towards my home on the hill,
The balloons held tightly in my hand,
Lest they fly into oblivion.
I gave one each to my brood of siblings
And, with our eyes shining,
We stepped out to play.
But, as you know,
Helium balloons need to be held tightly,
Lest they fly away
Much like our emotions, to our relationships,
To our life.
And, the moment I loosened my grip,
Off it flew into oblivion
There was sadness, albeit momentary
As I watched its flight.

And, that is life.
How ever much we try to hold on to things,
Yet, they have a measurement.
In time.
We should learn to enjoy the moment
And release.

Will you release your cultured balloons with me?
Or will you hold them tightly till you die?

People

All the water bottles in my house,
Disappear at night, into the nooks and corners,
Unseen, unknown.
Much like the people, who are their companions
In the nightly pursuits of travelling in abandon
The bottles become like the witches' brooms,
Going helter-skelter
As the mind travels with the speed of light,
To go to domains unseen and unheard.
And, these bottles become the friend, philosopher and guide
To take us individually,
On a path, where we fear to go
For in the light of the day,
We hold ourselves back,
And, put on a plastic smile,
To go on the journey of every day.
Dejected, morose, unhappy
But, as night falls, we are equipped for adventure,
With the bottle as a prop.
For, the many realms of the conscious mind,
Are not there.
And, we can sit in the wishing chair with the broom,
To fly into the unknown,
Within our mind.
As we learn to unpeel these layers, we reach the source.
And here, the illusory world ends.

We merge
The props fall.
The inside and the outside becomes one.

The Mirror

Divided into uneven segments, unlike the perfect ones from nature,
Caricatured,
Into various forms of my own making.
The mirror would, but show,
Various faces, contorted.
Much like the magic ones.
The layers formed,
Would divide and rule within.
The many creases on my forehead,
Would become like the undulating craters.
And, I would be lost, in a maze,
Similar to the of labyrinth of Abhimanyu.
He learnt the tricks, unborn.
And, so did I.
Through the many lifetimes,
Of birth, of death.
And, you were there,
Always,
Looking out for me,
Helping me see, through the unidimensional walls
Of faith,
Of truth,
Of surrender.
For you taught me all,
and, that,
Love is not blind,
The seer is.

For love is multidimensional
And, you exist,
Beyond,
Waiting, for me
To break the labyrinth,
And turn it into
A kaleidoscope,
Of color,
Of form,
To walk me home.
And merge,
With the source.

Freedom

How many cages have I been locked into?
How many cages have I locked myself into?
As I look through the bars,
I know not the difference
I am the same,
Behind them.
Rocking between being helpless and hopeful,
I look at others to help free me from the bondage.
Who is the prisoner here?
Who will set whom free?
Am I like the elephant,
Who,
Tied by a small rope,
Thinks he is chained.
He knows not the truth.
Am I within or without?
Who am I?

Memories

As the eyes mist up,
My thoughts go back wistfully,
As if looking through the mirrors,
Each one falls
And breaks into a million pieces,
The next one taking its place,
Slowly, they become congruent with my line of thought
Who says the past is past?
It is as vivid as the present,
I roam about in the whirlpool,
Confused, dejected,
Torn, helpless.
The centrifuge rises in its circular motion,
And I drown,
Slowly, into the abyss
My thoughts no longer in my control,
I become a watcher,
Of whom I was,
Before,
I became me.

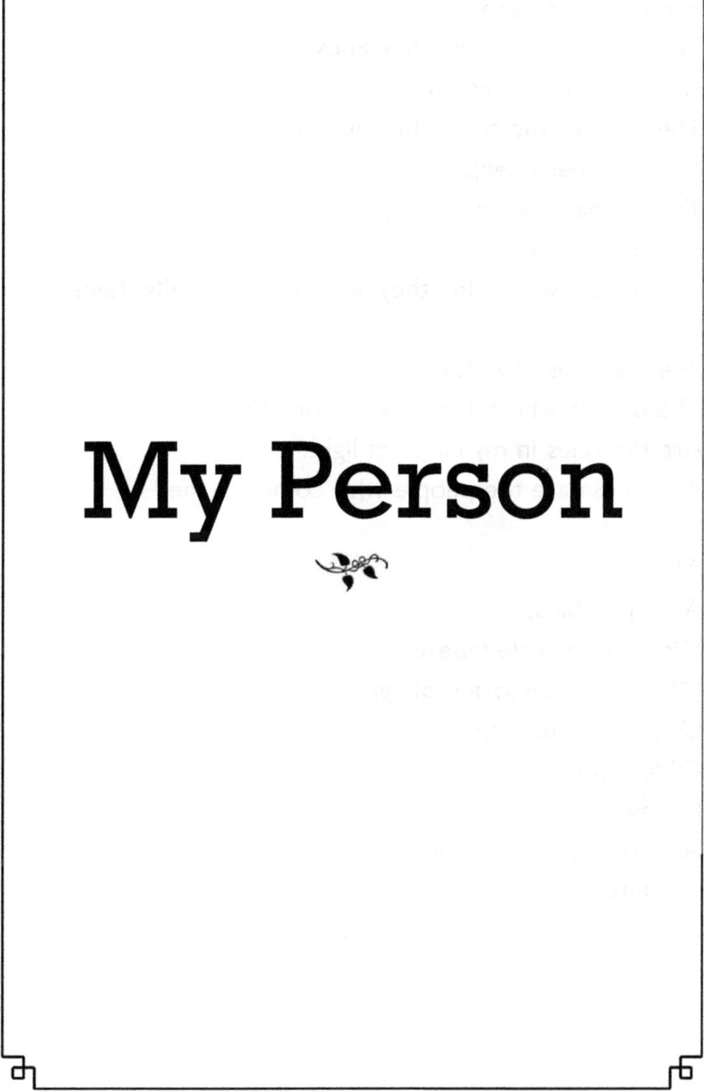

My Person

The people who think they want to know me,
Are the ones I seek.
The people who think they know me,
Are the ones I question.
The people who think they need me,
Are the ones I keep.
The people who think they cherish me,
Are the ones I love.
The people who think they are unconditionally there
for me,
Are the ones I live for.
The people who think they surround me,
Are the ones in my circle of light.
And, these are the people who complete me.
For I am,
After all,
A weaver bird,
Weaving my little tapestry
Of love, of memories, of light,
Of hope, of dreams
Of fulfillment
I weave,
A tapestry, full of colors,
In white.

Yet Again

Yet again I find myself broken,
Crevices, some filled, some oozing,
Wounded in parts, healed in some.
Impermanence is the way of life
But, knowledge does not mean knowing
Acceptance comes from within.
Yet again, the broken comes forward
And, I, cannot control its flow
Yet again, I fail
Yet again, I falter
Yet again, life recedes
And my hands are unable to form the cups,
To hold, to catch, to cherish
Yet again, the broken in me,
Wins.

The Dungeons

In the dark alleys,
The dungeons whereI have lived all my life,
Accustoming my eyes to see,
The sliver of light, which fell from the lamppost,
Enveloping the gray of the sky.
Lurking here and there,
Looking furtively to find a place to stay,
Slowly and steadily,
Like the tortoise.
Noiselessly,
Steadying its gait,
And plunking itself in a small nook.
Invisible to my strained eyes,
Which have had a veil on themfor so long.
A veil which I created myself,
To make it feel home and occupy,
Not only the nook,
But, every corner of me.
Entwining me in the web
Tightening me with its noose and slowly,
Making me suffocate,
In my own breath.
Till I am forced, to ask for my own death,
To liberate from its clutches.
It takes over my house,
The dark alleys, the dungeons,
Where I have lived forever,
And, throw me out.

I succumb and I die, a painful death.
The anaconda rises and swallows me whole.
I disappear, I am no more.
The sliver of light engulfs all of what I was.
I eat myself up.

The Checkerboard

We are the chequered forms
Of our own selves, with the other.
We sap into our energy, to give out,
But, we fail to channelize it directly.
We add color and spice to it
And present it with a lot of theatre
Distorting who we are

We know what we want to hear
But we fail, to listen to our inner voice
And listen, only to the commotion of our thoughts

We know what we want to see
But we fail, to see the truth
And see the projections of our mind

We know what we want to inhale
But we fail, to inhale the pure air
And fall for the adulterations

We know what we want to touch
But we fail, to touch the inner chord
And try and sing with the cacophony

We know what we want to taste
But we fail to taste the nectar
And fill our mouths with the poisons

We live in the outer senses
And fail to connect, with the inner ones.
We fail as a human
We become the checkerboard

A mix of the other
And, not our own self.
Only, if.

No Words

Words stop coming out, as my throat chokes
Whether out of emotion or fear, I am unable to
understand,
The emotion of being lost in translation
Or the fear of not being heard.

And, slowly my presence takes a life size form,
I follow the escape route,
Unable to explain anymore,
I become mute to the world,
And, progress in my journey,
Of becoming deaf as well.

Unbroken

The image broke
And, so did the mirror
A thousand pieces,
Shattered.
Pricking my being at the various vantage points,
I could not save my own self.
Broken, dejected
I fell on my knees.
The pain.
The hide and seek played on,
With the broken mirage of me,
As blood oozed out of the pores of my being,
I lied to myself
That I am alright
So, what if,
There will be scars all over,
Like the chicken pox.
Scaling my body
So, what if,
I would be left unattended,
Like the leftover food in the garbage can
I, of five star qualities, lied to my own self
That, I was made by bluer blood
That I did not get hurt
That, I was always in one piece
Whole,
In a million pieces

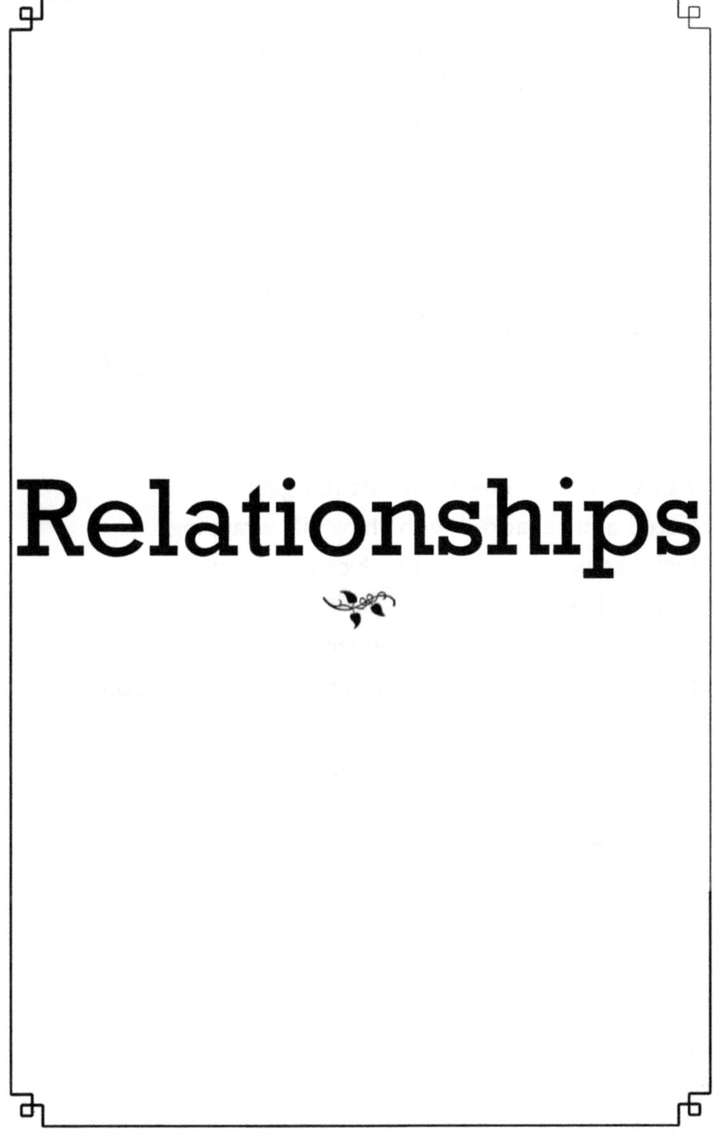

Relationships

As I got up in the morning,
Sleepily making my morning cup of tea,
My eyes went out to the terrace
Seeking my morning companion, the newspaper
A relationship developed over the years
The relationships we have are, myriad,
With our holy beads
Or with the water which the milkman puts,
The horn of the school bus,
Or with the dirt lying unattended in the nooks and corners
Relationships
With the annual Diwali, Christmas gifts
Dusted and repacked with shiny gift wrapping,
Much like we dress up ourselves everyday
Relationships
With the social media or the smart phone
Or with the dressing up of the body, minus the soul
Relationships
With the lifeless or with the living
Or with the self
Relationships
Out of habit
Or out of convenience
Out of love
Or hate
Relationships
For we are social
After all.

The Gift

I looked in wonderment
At the small box,
Lovingly wrapped,
With a bow of shiny ribbons.
With glitter strewn around
Neat, pretty,
With glossy paper.
What a feeling,
To receive a present
In the hope that,
It will be a pathway to your desire
How I wish that the giver would understand,
What I wanted?
Of course, without even voicing explicitly
If only, wishes were horses.
Slowly, with shaking fingers,
I started to open,
Not wanting to spoil the wrapping,
Or pull at the ribbon.
Like one would caress a loved one.
Inside was a beautiful blue box of velvet
Shining, glossy
With hope,
I prodded further,
And opened the little silver latch.
There were bits of paper inside,
All neatly arranged,
Something written on each one of them.

The choicest of abuses
The demeaning words
In black and white, of hurt,
Resentment and anger
The memories came flooding back
I smiled.
And I closed the box.
These were my medals.
For, I had moved on
And, they had helped me
Look past the past.

The Scale

On which weighing scale will you measure me?
What price will you put?
Against what will you weigh me?
Some ounces of sentences
Some desires
Some memories
But, these will be not sold in the markets
Still, you should keep trying,
My friend
It is easy, very easy
To find foes in the world
The problem is only with friends
Weigh all the treasure you want
But, you will find
That my side would still be way heavier
You know why?
Because,
I let you sculpt only my emptiness
Yes, only the emptiness
I did not let you touch my completeness
Neither were you capable enough of touching it
And that is why,
My dear friend
My side will always be heavier.

The Search

How much have I lived my life?
Have I lived more and less is left?
Or vice versa?
The dry leaves made a crunching sound
Below my feet
I looked for silence in those leaves
The same silence
Which one gets, when one walks on the fresh ones
But, it was the autumn of my life
And, I was searching for the spring
Through the lens of the changing seasons
I kept looking through
Like a silent spectator
I realized and learnt that
I am the same
The seasons will change
And, so will the relationships
As is their nature
Who am I?
But,
A spectator
Silent, still
At peace
Rooted.

The Ostrich

As I walked along the sea line
Lost in my thoughts
I cupped the clear water in my hands
Waiting for it to seep down
Through the gaps in my palms
I could not hold it
But I always thought that
I held my life tightly in my hands
It also fell, like these waters
I watched, silently
Trapped,
In a bond,
Which had putrefied
And had no meaning left
I wanted to tuck in the entire span
In my closed palms
Making the shape of a shell
Waiting to find that elusive pearl
Upon opening,
I resisted to change
Non acceptance to reality
I fell, face forward into the sand
The water merged with the ocean
I lay buried, in oblivion
Much like the ostrich
Mirage like.

Farewell

When the last rays of the sun
Shone through your sheer curtains,
They cast a magical glow on your face
The sun was about to set, and darkness bared its fangs
To engulf the room in which you lay,
In peace, within yourself
Having accepted, that there was little to do now
Very little effort left, just a few more breaths to take
You looked at the sun setting
And smiled inside,
Your soul aglow with the warmth and the love
You were finally going home
This earthly home came with its trials and tribulations
Which you fulfilled with grace,
With your head held high.
My only regret is that,
I wish I was there,
To watch this final sunset with you,
To bask in its warmth,
To go home with you.

Rejoice

Don't wait for me to go
Rejoice, for I am already gone.
I am in the thousand flowers that bloom,
The sun that shines anew,
The flowing waters of the ocean,
I am in you,
In the small breaths you take,
The little tears you hide,
The beautiful smiles you give in abandonment,
For I am a part of you, as you are of me,
You came through me or I through you,
The connection is more than the mortal lifetimes,
In me is the universe,
In you is me,
We merge in the divine
And, that is all there is,
Nothing more, nothing less
Just this infinite circle,
The unending, untiring hands of time,
Time, an illusion
Like me
Do I exist?
Who am I?
If not you?
Like the millions of pebbles, strewn on the banks,
Just another me, just another you.

Tribute

The relationship she had with you is gone,
Preserved like a mummy.
For she now glows
Like a star
Which she has become,
Showering her blessings still,
Like the unseen hand of God
Like the dance of the slow breeze
Like the warmth of the sun
Like the glimpse of her in you
And, in the others who loved her
Let her shine, let her live
In the many waters of the Ganga
Let her flow, through her many lifetimes
Some with you, some without
She was not yours to keep
Ever.
She was always of the flowing robes,
The salt pepper hair,
The angelic smile
But, you thought,
That she was yours to keep,
Forever.
As the relationship you had with her,
You did not let go
For fear of losing her
But, she was never yours in the first place
She had to fly to unknown destinations

And, you became selfish
And, caught her to keep in a cage
Let her go.
For she needs to blossom
And, so do you
For, you are her fellow traveller
And, not her captor
Play the role you have
Don't play the role of the other
For this assignment is ours to complete
Do the task well
And, move on
Like she did
At peace.

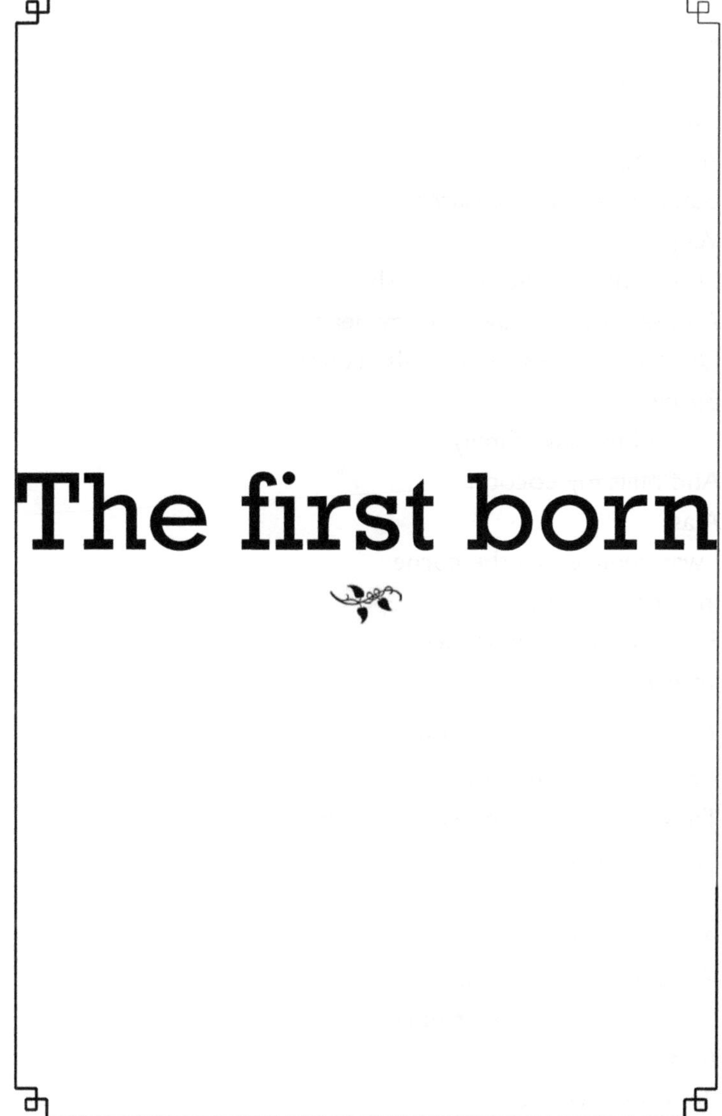

The first born

I was the first born,
A male at that
The cynosure of eyes
I was the bully
To all my siblings
But, became the patriarch
Very early
I took this role very seriously
And sat with a crown on my head
Ordering the lesser mortals around
Bit by bit,
I raised my own family
And built my cocoon
Alas,
I was reduced to the corner
In my own house
For lack of independence
To my children

As they say, heaven and hell
Are here on earth only
They are not in the sky or the sea
In that corner,
I stayed,
Alone, lost, uncared.
With food passed on,
Like it is to a prisoner in jail
And, where, I
Breathed my last
Today.

My Dad's Chair

It stood erect, on its sturdy feet
The weather had put its stamp here and there
But it spoke volumes without uttering
The toothache, the ice cream dollop
The standing up on little feet
The handles which felt like climbing up the Himalayas
Life, a perspective
From the eye
Of curled up sleep
Of lazy afternoons in the lap
Of wonderment at the stories being read out
Of a bespectacled figure, bending down
Working furiously, intently
Of laughter, of love, of sharing
Ah!
Memories.
What would we do without them?
They make life worth living
Each moment was etched within
As I sat on it
A relic which equaled me in age only
But, had lived more lives
A masterpiece
My Dad's chair, in front of me
I do have a very big seat
To fill.

Passing By

Like a whisper in the ear,
Like a caress on the cheek,
Like a gentle touch of hand,
Surreptitiously.
It walks,
No trumpets are blown
No sounds are heard
I get goose bumps
As it passes me by,
No knock on the door
No words uttered
None listened to..
It walks,
After touching my soul
Leaving me wet
By its elixir
Momentarily.

I stand lost,
In one place
Unable to figure
The going and the coming
Because,
I am closed by the many walls around me,
A carcass
And, life
Comes and goes
Taking my soul with it.

My Past

My past became my present, slowly,
Yet steadily
Some dead leaves, strewn here and there
Some logs, depicting age with their concentric circles
Some challenges, some tests
Some destinations, some paths
Some broken relationships, some happy moments

My past..
I kept watering the dead,
hoping to see a sliver of life
But, no new leaves sprouted
Neither did any flowers bloom

My past..
Kept on looking at me
Through a dusty mirror
And trapped in the dust
I died
In the desire
Of a tomorrow.

Death/Life

How do I want to die?
Do I want to die a life full of bitterness?
Resentment, ego, anger?
Do I want to never let go?
Do I want to fulfill all my desires?
Do I want to keep living in the past and, also the future?
Do I want..?
What do I really want?
Do I really even know what I want..?

I think of the time elapsed and the time yet to come
I think of the sunrises and the sunsets
I think of how much I have lived
But, time is an illusion, as is life or death.
I do not die
Neither do I live

9 789386 148018

Printed by Libri Plureos GmbH in Hamburg, Germany